W9-ARD-351

DISCARD

JF YOUNG
Young, Jessica (Jessica E.)
A magic spark.

1920
on1110145321 12/08/2020

A Magic Spark

Read more
Fairylight Friends!

Fairylight Friends
A Magic Spark

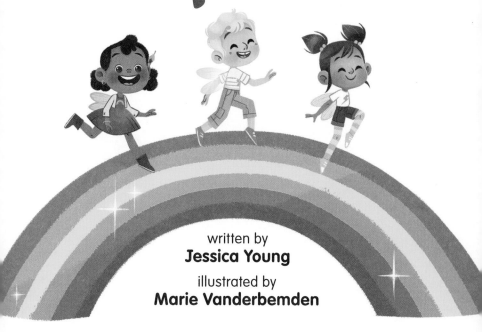

written by
Jessica Young

illustrated by
Marie Vanderbemden

ACORN™
SCHOLASTIC INC.

For Kate, who helped me find my magic —JY

For Lio, for all the love, laughs, encouragement, and coffee you bring me every day —MV

Text copyright © 2020 by Jessica Young

Illustrations copyright © 2020 by Marie Vanderbemden

Library of Congress Cataloging-in-Publication Data

Names: Young, Jessica (Jessica E.), author. | Vanderbemden, Marie, illustrator.
Title: A magic spark / Jessica Young ; illustrations by Marie Vanderbemden.
Description: First edition. | New York : Acorn/Scholastic Press, 2020. |
Series: Fairylight friends | Summary: Ruby, Iris, and Pip first met on their first day of fairy school, and they immediately became best friends, testing their wings, and enjoying their magical adventures—but sometimes it takes a little time for a fairy to find her true magic spark.
Identifiers: LCCN 2019027460 | ISBN 9781338596526 (paperback) |
ISBN 9781338596533 (library binding)
Subjects: LCSH: Fairies—Juvenile fiction. | Fairies—Juvenile fiction. |
Magic—Juvenile fiction. | Best friends—Juvenile fiction. | CYAC:
Fairies—Fiction. | Magic—Fiction. | Best friends—Fiction. |
Friendship—Fiction.
Classification: LCC PZ7.Y8657 Mag 2020 | DDC 813.6 [E]—dc23
LC record available at https://lccn.loc.gov/2019027460

10 9 8 7 6 5 4 3 2 1   20 21 22 23 24

Printed in China   62
First edition, September 2020

Edited by Katie Carella
Book design by Maria Mercado

Table of Contents

Map of Fairy Forest

Sunset
Meadow

Wishing
Bridge

Fairy Berry
Patch

Crystal Pool

Lily
Pond

Fairy
School

Miss Goldwing's
House

Moon
Lake

Iris's House

Ruby's House

Pip's
House

Meet the Fairylight Friends

Ruby

Pip

Iris

The Magic Pool

Ruby, Iris, and Pip were fairy friends. They loved going to fairy school.

Ruby loved making art.

Ta-da!

Iris loved flying fast.

Wheee!

BOING!

Pip loved growing things.

Group hug!

At school, the friends practiced their fairy moves.

They tiptoed.

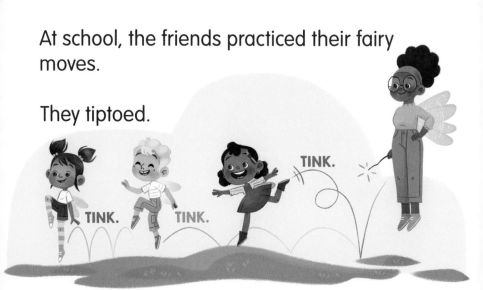

TINK.

TINK.   TINK.

They flew.

ZIP!

ZIP!

ZIP!

One day, their teacher, Miss Goldwing, shared some exciting news.

We're going on a field trip!

Where?

You'll see.
Follow me!

The friends tiptoed across Wishing Bridge.

They flew through Fairy Forest.

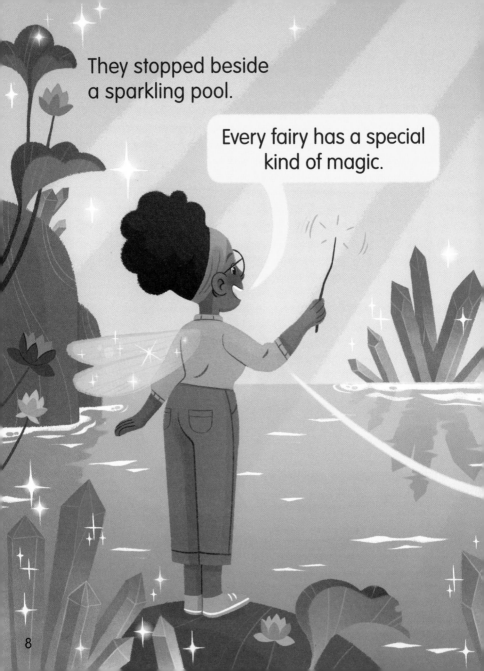

They stopped beside
a sparkling pool.

Every fairy has a special
kind of magic.

8

BLUB-BLUB-BLUB. Ruby, Iris, and Pip each saw a different picture in the pool.

A rainbow!

A lightning bolt!

A flower!

The Cake

Pip was flying by Ruby's house. He heard some loud noises.

CLANG!
BANG!
CRASH!

Ruby was in the kitchen.

15

Ruby sifted the flour.

A while later, Pip came back.

Is the cake done?

Not yet. Will you help me crack the eggs?

That sounds fun. But I have to stretch my wings.

Ruby cracked the eggs.

CRACK!
CRACK!

Pip came back again.

Ruby beat the batter and poured it into a pan.

She put the pan into the oven.

Soon the cake was baked. Ruby frosted it.

She showered it with sprinkles. There was a puff of pink fairy dust!

Sprinkle, sprinkle!

TWINKLE-TWINKLE!

Suddenly, the cake was beautiful!

21

Yay! I found my magic!

Just then, Pip showed up.

Wow! That looks amazing!

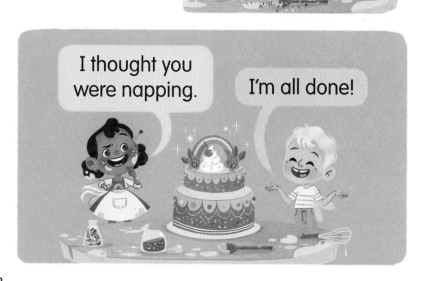

I thought you were napping.

I'm all done!

22

YUM!

MMM.

Star in a Jar

Ruby, Iris, and Pip were looking at the stars.

Iris had an idea.

Iris packed
a snack.

Iris put on
her coat.

Then she took off in a puff of blue fairy dust.

I'll wave from the moon!
Vroom! Vroom!

Go, Iris, go!

zoooooo

She found
her magic!

Iris flew higher and higher.

She flew until she was too tired to fly.

Then she tumbled like a falling leaf.

She fell faster and faster.

Iris slipped off her coat.

The coat puffed up. Iris drifted down.

It's a good thing we're happy right where we are.

34

The Seeds

Iris was out for her morning fly. She flew
to Pip's house.

Pip was in the garden.

I love their bright colors!

I love their sweet smell!

I love their soft petals!

38

Iris and Pip watched the soil.

Your flowers are not growing.

Yes, they are.

No, they are not.

Are.

Not.

Just wait. They grow slow.

Iris could not wait.

Grow! Grow! Grow!
Go! Go! Go!

Pip tried to help his flowers grow.

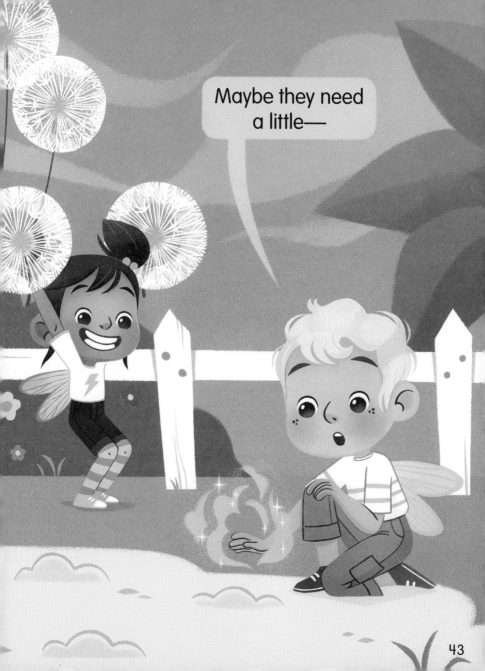

Maybe they need
a little—

43

45

Surprise Party

Ruby, Iris, and Pip were picking berries.

FAIRY
BERRY PATCH

We have so many berries.
We should share them!

Ruby thought of a fun plan.

Let's throw a party!

We can use our magic and surprise Miss Goldwing!

Pip did a flip.

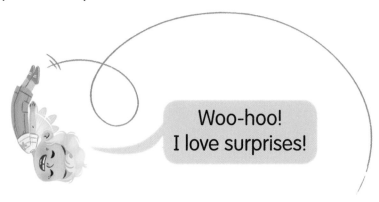

Woo-hoo! I love surprises!

Ruby, Iris, and Pip got ready for the party.

Ruby made things fancy.

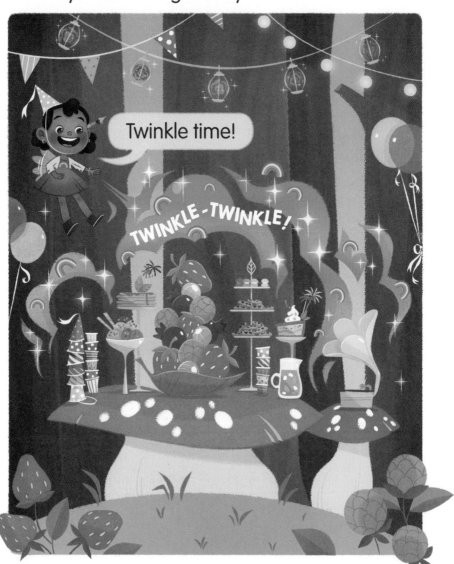

Iris raced to find their forest friends.

Pip grew some flowers.

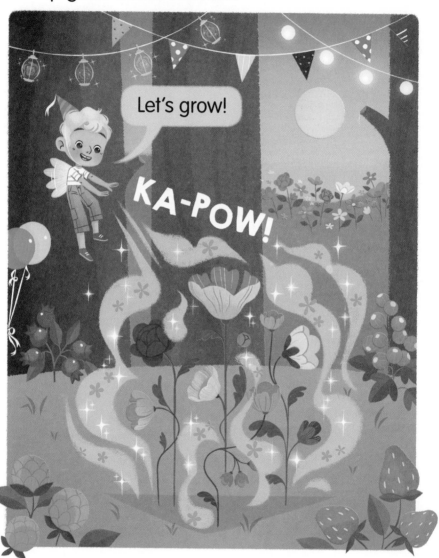

Just as the sun set, the friends spotted Miss Goldwing.

About the Creators

JESSICA YOUNG grew up in Ontario, Canada. When she's not making up stories, she loves making art with kids. Her other books include the Haggis and Tank Unleashed early chapter book series, the Finley Flowers series, *Play This Book*, *Pet This Book*, *Spy Guy The Not-So-Secret Agent*, and *My Blue Is Happy*.

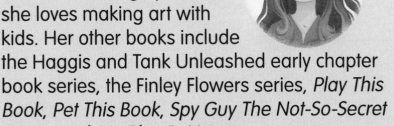

MARIE VANDERBEMDEN works from her barge moored in Belgium. Telling stories through drawing has always been her passion. Marie has worked mainly in the illustration of children's books and animated movies. Fairylight Friends is the first early reader series she has illustrated. When she is not sketching, she also enjoys photography, sculpture, and teaching ceramics.

YOU CAN DRAW RUBY!

1. Draw three shapes for Ruby's head and dress.

2. Add two ears, arms, and legs.

3. Draw Ruby's hair and shoes.

4. Draw one rainbow, one paintbrush, and two wings.

5. Add Ruby's face, earrings, knees, and jacket details.

6. Color in your drawing!

WHAT'S YOUR STORY?

Ruby, Iris, and Pip each have a special kind of magic. If **you** were a fairy, what kind of magic would you have? How would you find your magic spark? (Think about things you love to do—or things you'd like to try!) Write and draw your story!